LIANG and the MAGIC PAINTBRUSH

by DEMI

Holt, Rinehart and Winston / *New York*

To Jesse

Library of Congress Cataloging in Publication Data
Demi.   Liang and the magic paintbrush.
SUMMARY: A poor boy who longs to paint is given
a magic brush that brings to life whatever he pictures.
[1. Painting—Fiction.   2. Magic—Fiction]
I. Title.   PZ7.D3925Li   [E]   80-11351
ISBN 0-03-056289-9

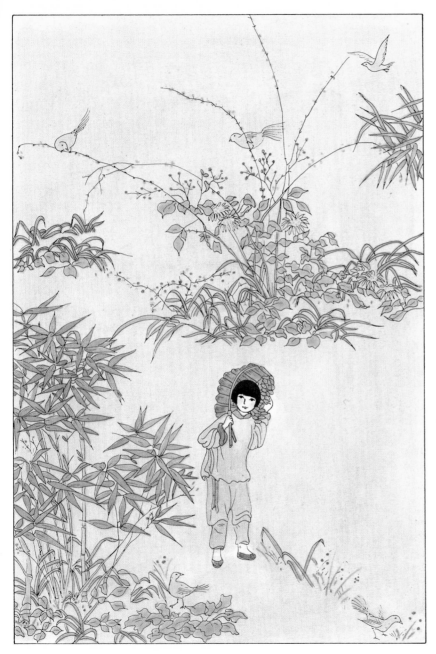

Long ago in China, a boy named Liang earned money gathering firewood and cutting reeds. His one wish was to paint. But he could not afford to buy a brush.

One day he passed an art
school and went in. "I want so
much to paint," he said.
"Please, will you teach me?"

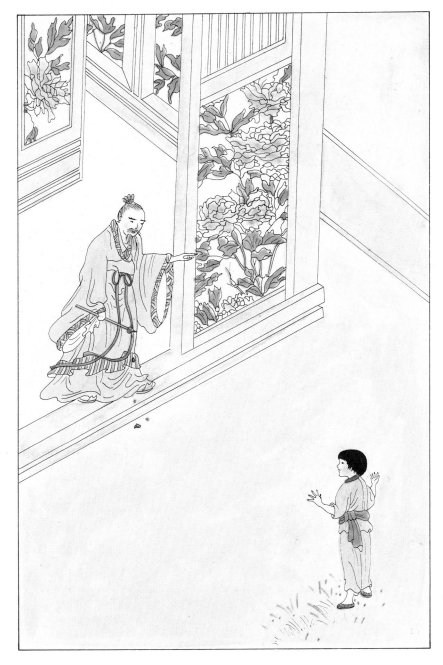

"What!" The teacher glared at him. "A beggar wants to paint?" He drove Liang away.

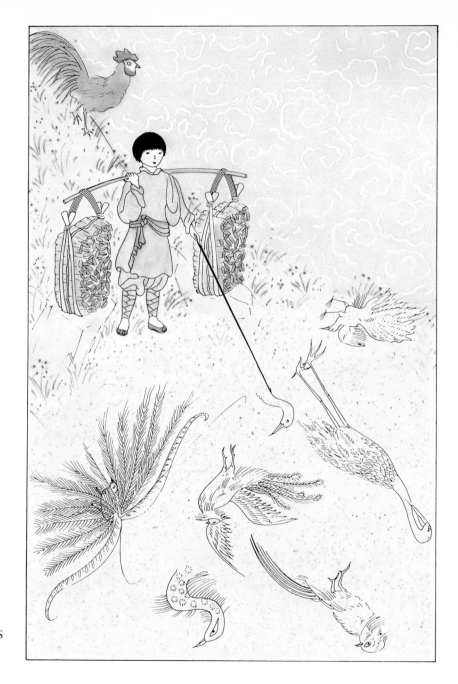

But Liang could not keep his fingers still. When he went to gather firewood he drew birds in the sand with a twig.

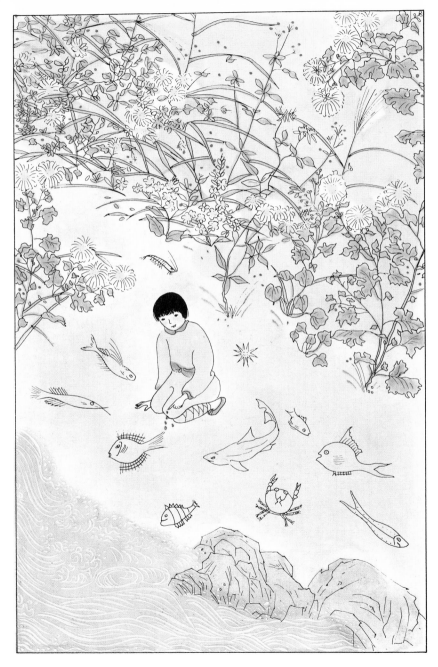

When he went to the river to cut reeds he drew fish on the rocks with drops of water.

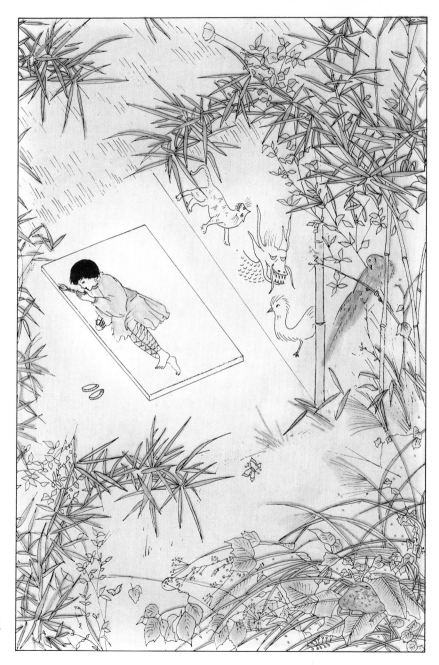

One night as he slept an old man appeared on a phoenix and placed a brush in Liang's hand.

"It is a magic paintbrush. Use it carefully," the old man said and flew away.

Liang jumped for joy. "Thank you so much!" he called after the old man. Immediately Liang began to paint.

He painted deer. As he finished, he saw that the deer came to life. It really was a magic paintbrush!

"I will paint things for my poor friends," he thought. And he painted toy birds, horses, lanterns, and balls for the children.

And for their parents, things to cook with, furniture for the house, and tools for the field.

Then he went to the market-
place and set up a table among
the other merchants. And
he made pictures of birds to
sell. To make sure the birds
did not come to life, he left
something out.

One day a man asked for a picture of a crane. Liang gave it only one eye. But by accident, one drop of ink fell where the second eye should have been — and the crane flew away.

Now everyone knew about Liang's magic brush. Including the greedy emperor.

He went out with all his soldiers
to take the brush away from
Liang.

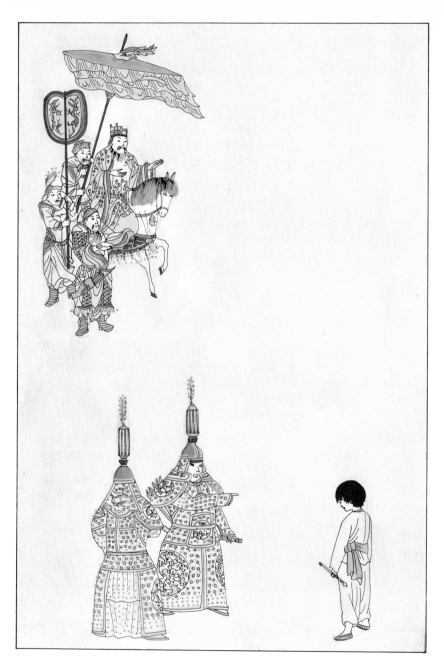

But Liang refused to give it up.

The emperor ordered him bound and brought to the palace.

There the emperor ordered Liang to paint a dragon. But Liang painted a toad instead. The emperor then ordered him to paint a phoenix. He painted a rooster instead.

Furious, the emperor seized the brush and ordered Liang imprisoned. The greedy emperor then sat down to paint mountains of gold. But they turned into rocks and rolled off the table.

The emperor tried again. He painted a large tree. But what do you think happened? It turned into an enormous python which nearly bit the emperor's head off.

Liang knew the brush would lose its magic in the emperor's hands. He thought of a plan. And he sent word to the emperor saying that in exchange for his freedom he would paint whatever the emperor wished. The emperor accepted.

"Paint me the sea," the emperor
ordered. Liang drew a sea.
"Where are the fish?" the
emperor asked.

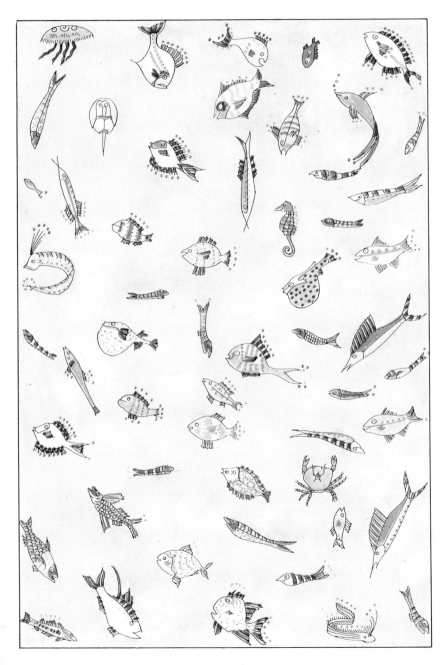

Liang drew and drew and soon
a sea full of fish were swimming
about.

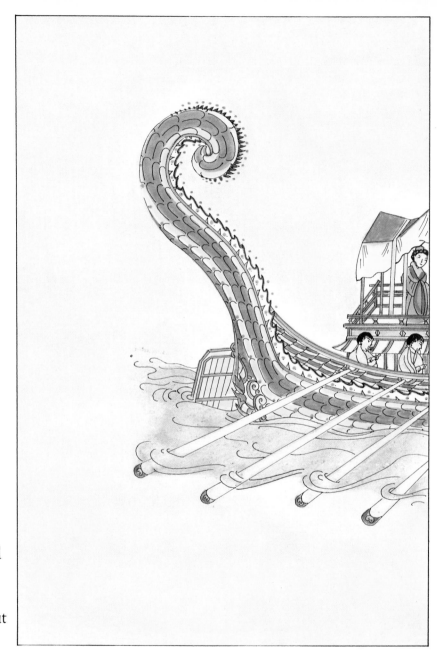

"So long as we have a sea," said the emperor, "let us have a boat!" Liang painted a boat, which was soon bobbing about on the water.

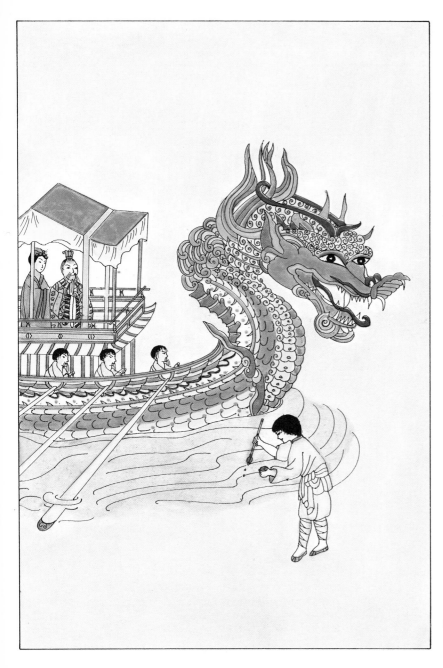

Delighted, the emperor
called the royal family to come
and join him on the boat.

"Get us some wind, so we can move," cried the emperor. Happily, Liang painted wind and the boat began to rock. "More wind!" the emperor cried. Liang drew more wind, and more. Soon waves were splashing and crashing over the deck.

"Enough!" the emperor cried.
But Liang would not listen.
He drew so much wind, the
boat keeled over and broke into
a million pieces. The emperor
and the royal family sank to the
bottom of the sea.

The story of Liang and his magic paintbrush spread far and wide. But what became of Liang? Nobody knows.

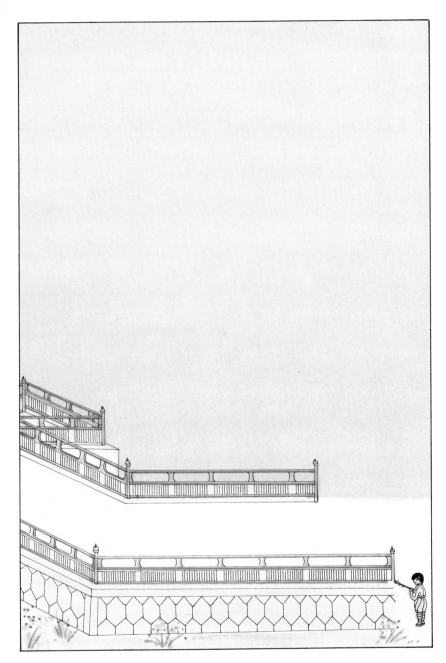

Some say that he went back to his own village. Others say that he roamed the earth painting for the poor wherever he went.

About the Author

A student of Corita Kent in California, Demi has traveled and studied art throughout the world. She has received several art awards, including a Fulbright Scholarship to study in India, and her diverse range of work has been exhibited from coast to coast and even abroad. Among the mediums she works in are serigraph, watercolor, mobile, collage, and textile design. The author and/or illustrator of numerous well-received children's books and magazine articles, she makes her home in New York City.